Christina Sorino 2008

An Orphan's Promise

A Christmas Story

By
Dan T. Davis

Illustrated by
Christina E. Siravo

Edited by Jan Davis

Second Star Creations

An Orphan's Promise
By Dan T. Davis
Illustrated by Christina E. Siravo
Edited by Jan Davis
Design & Layout by Jani Duncan Smith, It Girl Design
Published by: Second Star Creations
12120 State Line Rd #190, Leawood, KS 66209-1254
http://www.secondstar.us
Email to: ordersOP@secondstar.us

Text copyright © 2006 by Dan T. Davis
Illustrations copyright © 2006 by Second Star Creations
Printed in China
First Edition

10 9 8 7 6 5 4 3 2 1
Publisher's Cataloging-in-Publication
(Provided by Quality Books, Inc.)

Davis, Dan T., 1957-
   An orphan's promise : a Christmas story / by Dan T. Davis ;
illustrated by Christina E. Siravo. — 1st ed.
   p. cm.
   SUMMARY: In 1910 Norway, an orphan girl arrives at
Santa's workshop. Mr. and Mrs. Kloss teach her how to
make toys and to always keep her promises.
      Audience: Ages 7-12.
      LCCN: 2005909609
      ISBN-13: 978-0-9725977-5-3
      ISBN-10: 0-9725977-5-1

1. Orphans—Juvenile fiction. 2. Promises—Juvenile
fiction. 3. Santa Claus—Juvenile fiction. [1. Orphans
—Fiction. 2. Promises—Fiction. 3. Santa Claus—
Fiction. 4. Christmas—Fiction.]   I. Siravo, Christina
E. II. Title.

PZ7.D28583Orp 2006   [Fic]
                              QBI06-600144

*Dedicated to
those who have touched our lives...*

CHAPTERS

ARRIVAL

Ruby stood alone on the high road, overlooking the Norwegian village where Santa Kloss lived. Shivering, she drew her worn coat closely around her.

The feed wagon she'd arrived in dwindled into the distance. Ruby let out a heavy sigh, fetched the small bag the driver had thrown to the ground, and began her downhill trek toward the village.

Kicking a rock in front of her, Ruby considered each building in the distance. "Now I have to figure out which house Santa Kloss lives in."

At the first house, she saw an older man with his teenage daughter carrying the day's goods. Ruby walked quickly past them without speaking.

"Little girl?" called the teenager.

Ruby walked faster. "Don't chase me," she thought. She kept looking over her shoulder, but the two said nothing more.

"I have to keep going. I have to find Mr. Kloss." Ruby had heard so much about his kindness. Maybe he'd be different from all the others.

It had taken all summer to convince the headmistress of her orphanage to let her come, but now that she was here, doubts she'd refused to think about began to creep in. "What if even Santa Kloss turns me away?" Ruby fretted. "She said he wouldn't take me in, but she didn't mind me leaving."

Ruby noticed a little color on the roadside. "Maybe Mr. Kloss would like flowers…" As she gathered the pretty weeds, Ruby winced at a large bruise on her left side. "I wonder if the orphanage would even take me back?"

Ruby reached into her pocket and felt three small coins, the last remnants of four years of odd jobs. Her stomach grumbled.

Panic gripped her as she considered returning. She had enough money for a little bread, but travel would have to be begged, as the headmistress had arranged her travel only one way.

"I'm not going back. Mr. Kloss just has to take me in. He loves kids. That's why he makes toys!"

Ruby spied a house and barn across from the village's small church. The house displayed a carpenter's sign; the barn door had a carved sleigh filled with toys above it.

"That's it!" she declared.

Ruby's smile turned to a frown as she smoothed the coat covering her dirty dress and scuffed shoes. "But it's my only good dress," she worried. "And I haven't gotten all the straw out of my hair!"

As she fussed with her clothes, she gasped as her present of colorful weeds scattered across the village road. She stared at her empty hands, thinking, "I don't have anything to give him."

She heard a noise and her eyes darted back to the barn. The door opened and a man in his fifties began to walk out, carrying a water bucket. He had reddish hair that had turned mostly silver, with a beard that held hints of red as well. He was a big man, with large muscular arms showing how hard he worked on whatever task he took on. He stopped, surprised, as he saw Ruby staring at him.

Ruby rushed toward him and gulped as she hurriedly took out her letter of introduction. Holding it out, she breathlessly said, "Mr. Kloss, my name is Ruby Hjort, and I heard you take in orphans and teach them carpentry, and I'd really love to learn a trade, and I can help you build toys, and I work hard, and I do good work, and everyone at my orphanage says I get things done, and I always work with a smile, and I'm willing to do whatever you need, and..."

Ruby was interrupted by a loud, long laugh. "Oh ho ho! Slow down, slow down, little one. And come in, before we both catch our death of cold."

He motioned her in, closed the door, and continued. "Ruby, is it? Well, first of all, everyone calls me Papa, so call me Papa. And I'm sure you work hard, but you must understand I teach carpentry as a trade to boys. In return, they make the toys that I give to children on Christ's day."

Ruby looked around the shop. Eight boys were diligently hammering, sawing, or painting some toy they had created. As the boys noticed Ruby looking at them, silence began to fill the room.

"What?" asked Papa. "You've never seen a girl before? Boys, this is Ruby Hjort. Ruby, these are my carpenter apprentices."

Ruby was sure that two of the boys scowled at her. Three quietly said hello. Papa said encouragingly, "Ok, boys, it's about time for a break, so let's see how the toys look."

As Papa walked Ruby through the toyshop, he complimented each boy's work. His kind words put a smile on every face.

Ruby gasped as she realized that these were some of the most wondrous wooden toys she had ever seen. She marveled at toys made for girls and boys of almost any age. "They're beautiful," said Ruby.

"It's early yet. Wait till it's near Christ's day," said Papa. "With eight boys, we almost fill the toyshop."

Finishing the tour, Papa began to lead Ruby back to the front door. "They're good boys. They're hard workers," Papa said to Ruby, obviously intending the boys to hear as well.

Papa continued, "But you can see I don't have a place for a girl, even one as pretty as you."

Ruby blushed at Mr. Kloss's compliment, but realized he wasn't going to accept her. "Why won't you take girls? I know I can learn carpentry!"

"Why, because I, because..." Papa laughed loudly again. "You know, little one, I've never really thought about it. It's just that the boys do the carpentry and the girls do the sewing. At least, that's how I've always known it."

Papa opened the door and looked out toward the roadway. He looked back at Ruby and asked, "Who brought you here? Do you need me to walk you to where you are staying?"

Ruby's eyes filled with tears. Even Santa was sending her away.

"Please, Mr. Kloss," Ruby whispered. She took two coins out of her pocket and raised them toward him. "I'm here by myself. I don't really have anywhere to go. Could I at least have some food before I try to get back to my orphanage?"

Mr. Kloss looked down at the little girl and gently closed her fingers back around the coins. "Of course. Let's go see Mama. She'll know what we should do."

Papa pointed to a side doorway exiting the toyshop. The two of them walked under a covered walkway toward Papa's home.

As they entered, he asked, "Which orphanage did you say you were from? I haven't forgotten to come there, have I? I try to visit at least four orphanages or hospitals each year now that I have more toys."

As Ruby answered, Papa's eyebrows rose. "That's quite a distance. I haven't been there myself yet, though I was hoping to go there at some point. You came here by yourself? At your age, your size?"

Ruby clasped her hands behind her back. "I'm... I'm eleven. Almost twelve!" Ruby lied. Quickly, she continued, "I came alone, but don't worry, I was always with people I knew... or at least someone my headmistress knew. I had to wait for when others were ready to go, so it did take four days..."

Ruby's stomach growled loudly. "But, I... I had enough food, and everyone was kind and helpful."

Papa looked concerned, but simply said, "And you'll have the same kindness here as well, I assure you." They stepped through the side entry, past a room containing a large dining table, and into the kitchen area of Papa's home.

"Mama! I've brought a new guest. Come see! Come see!"

Mama's presence filled the room. She was a tall woman whose age was hidden by the smoothness of her skin. It was hard to believe she was over fifty.

She appeared surprised that Papa had brought a girl into the house, but only for a moment. Her calmness balanced Papa's excitement as she asked, "And what is your name, my dear?"

Ruby looked up at Mr. and Mrs. Kloss. She felt tiny next to them; although she knew she wasn't overly small. Still, their kindness and concern filled the room.

With renewed hope, she said, "My name is Ruby, Mrs. Kloss..."

Papa whispered, "Mama. Call her Mama. Everyone does."

Ruby ignored him, knowing she had to win over Mama. "I'd heard Mr. Kloss taught orphans, and I wanted to learn carpentry from him. I may not be big, but I'm strong, and I've been told I have a good eye and a steady hand for detailed work."

Mama smiled. "And did he accept you, Ruby?" Mama looked to Papa and waited. Ruby silently crossed her fingers.

Papa looked back and forth between Mama and Ruby. "She said she was hungry, Mama. But if she really wants to stay…"

"Could she work with you, Mama? You could use help with the sewing and stuffing on some of the toys…" Papa stopped, not sure what else to say.

Mama looked at Ruby. "Did you come to learn sewing or woodworking? What do you want to do?"

"I guess I wanted to learn carpentry and make toys. But I know how to sew; I'll do whatever you need."

"Papa, she just wants to belong. Can't you teach her some carpentry? She can help me out, but children need to learn new things."

Papa laughed. "Of course, of course! I can teach her. She can learn. But she can help you out as well. You could use the help; we're making a lot of toys that need fabric here and there."

Mama nodded. "Ruby, you'll have to sleep here in the kitchen since you can't sleep in the barn upstairs with the boys. You can store your clothes on two of the pantry shelves."

Ruby grinned, realizing she could stay. Even if she only sewed and helped around the house, it was a start.

Ruby's stomach was gratified by a wonderful dinner. The boys were surprised to find her joining them at the dining table, but listened politely as Papa announced that Ruby would be working with Mama.

As the evening ended, Ruby helped Mama place a mattress and comforter within the open area underneath the kitchen stairs.

"I'll help with the sewing tomorrow," said Ruby.

"Ah, yes, the sewing," said Mama. "Or maybe something else." Mama's smile and a knowing wink convinced a tired Ruby that she'd soon be learning carpentry.

TEASING

"Ruby, your work area will be at this table with Rolf," said Daniel, the oldest of Papa's apprentices. "Rolf came here only four months ago, so you and he can learn together."

"You really should have come earlier," Daniel continued, "because spring and summer is when you learn carpentry. We build tables and chairs, repair just about everything, and do most of our wood carving then."

"You really shouldn't have come at all," said Leif. "A girl can't do carpentry, right, Vic?" Leif and Viktor whispered while Daniel and Ruby walked through the shop.

Daniel ignored them. "This is Dag and this is Peter. They've been here almost as long as I have. Papa used to do carpentry only for this village, but now many villages use us. I think people like how we use any extra money we earn to make toys and that Papa trains orphan boys to be carpenters."

Ruby heard Viktor whisper loudly, "Well, at least she looks like a boy…"

Daniel continued, "Here are our favorite brothers, Christopher and Kristian. They came here three years ago after Papa visited their orphanage."

Christopher looked up and said hello, but his brother just sat carving an owl. After a few moments, Kristian looked up shyly at Ruby and murmured, "Everyone calls me Cupid because I really like bows and arrows."

Daniel directed Ruby to her spot next to Rolf and left her there. Ruby looked over the set of tools that Mr. Kloss and Daniel had assembled for her. She picked up a hammer and then a small carving tool.

She looked around the toyshop and saw all the boys staring at her, knowing that she had no idea what to do next. After a short time, she stood and returned to the house, hearing loud laughter as she left.

As the days passed, Ruby worked mostly with Mama. Ruby ran errands, helped with the meals, fed the few animals that Papa and Mama kept, and swept the toyshop each day.

Ruby didn't mind the work, but loved how Mr. Kloss and Daniel began teaching her carpentry skills, even if the lessons were rare compared to her other tasks.

"I'm not very good yet," lamented Ruby.

"Not very good? Oh, ho ho! You're a bit impatient, I'd say. You've only been here three weeks, and already you want to be a master carpenter?" Mr. Kloss turned to Daniel and Rolf, who were watching Papa give Ruby a carving lesson.

Daniel replied, "Actually, she's a fast learner. A keen eye for detail, too. You may be frustrating her by giving the same lessons and items to make as you give Rolf."

Ruby replied, "I don't mind. What I do mind is when pieces of my project disappear. Or that day when the hammer was glued to the table. Or remember last week when my chair fell apart when I sat in it?"

Rolf jumped in. "Maybe you're learning too fast. Look at the dolphin you're making. You're already almost as good as me."

Ruby frowned. "Or maybe you boys are just mean." She noted the look that all three gave her. "Well, not you or Rolf, Daniel, I just meant... oh, never mind."

The next day, Ruby was headed to the market, but made her usual pass through the barn. She found herself staring at her wooden dolphin; paint had been sloppily poured all over it and her section of the worktable. She shouted out to the entire toyshop, "Why can't you leave me alone! You're orphans, too! You know what it's like to be left out and alone!"

"Ah, we didn't do it!" lied Viktor. "The barn elf did it!"

"The Nissen?" Ruby responded. "The barn elf wouldn't play tricks on me! The Nissen knows I'd give him pudding whenever he wanted it."

Viktor didn't answer, but just held the paint remover high above her head, so she had to stand on tiptoes to try to reach it.

"I need that!" sniffed Ruby. Knowing she was about to cry, she instead rapidly said, "Why do you tease me? You don't tease Cupid, even though he's the shortest. You don't tease Rolf, even though he's the new boy! Why don't any of you like me?"

She suddenly jumped to grab the can from Viktor, but Leif grabbed her arm and held her back. Ruby started crying as she shouted, "Let me go!"

Rolf spoke up. "Come on, Leif, Vic, let her go. She's not here much anyway. She does help Mama clean and cook for us. If we tease her too much, she might put too much pepper in our food."

Daniel appeared, stepped into the fray, and took the paint remover from Viktor. He set it on Ruby and Rolf's table next to the dolphin. "Let's get back to work," he simply said.

As Ruby and Rolf walked around toward their table, Ruby nimbly avoided Viktor's outstretched leg. She tried to resist sticking her tongue out at him, but she didn't succeed.

Daniel looked at the paint splotched dolphin and said, "Rolf, Ruby has Mama's list, so she can't fix the dolphin right now. Can you clean it for her?"

Rolf nodded. "Sure. Maybe now Ruby won't over-pepper my food."

Ruby whispered, "Thanks, Rolf. I'm glad someone is willing to help me."

"Don't thank me too much," Rolf whispered. "I have to get along with everyone, too. I tell jokes about you in the bunks upstairs with the rest of them."

"You tell jokes about me?" asked Ruby, trying her best not to cry.

"Think about it," said Rolf. "If I didn't, don't you think I'd be teased as much as you since I'm the new boy?"

"Oh! Ok. Still, thank you, I guess." Ruby watched as Rolf grabbed a rag to remove the paint.

"I hope I don't have to sand it again," sighed Rolf. "At least nothing was broken on it." He turned away from Ruby as he began to work.

Anxiously, Ruby left on her errand, hoping Rolf could save the dolphin.

That night, Mama checked on Ruby in her bed under the kitchen staircase. "Is everything ok, Ruby?" Mama asked.

Ruby murmured, "Yes, Mama, I'm fine."

"Are you sure, Ruby? Something seems wrong."

Ruby leaned up on her pillow. "Mama, I've been here almost a month now and I still don't have any friends. The boys don't like me, and I've been too busy to make friends with anyone in the village."

"Aren't I your friend?" asked Mama. "And Papa is your friend, too."

"Oh, yes, you and Mr. Kloss have been wonderful. I just meant friends, not grown-ups."

Mama checked the kitchen stove for the night's heat as she said, "I heard about what Daniel and Rolf did today. Aren't they your friends?"

"Maybe," said Ruby. "Daniel's almost a grown-up though. And Rolf tells jokes about me. But maybe I should make Rolf a present so he'll like me."

"If Rolf is your friend, you don't need a present to make him like you," replied Mama. Mama adjusted the covers around Ruby's neck and tucked them under the mattress. "Good night, Ruby."

"Good night, Mama."

CELEBRATION

As Christ's day neared, Ruby found she was no longer teased in the toyshop – Daniel made sure everyone stayed busy making toys. The teasing did continue, but it usually came during school lessons or when the weather allowed for play outside.

It was sunny the week before Christ's day, so the boys all went to play in the park. Ruby decided to avoid their taunts and jokes, so she fed the barn animals, milked the cow, and then played alone in the woods behind the house. She was throwing snowballs at a tree when she saw Mr. Kloss carrying a salt lick and an axe out into the wild. She pulled her coat tighter and rushed after him. "Where are you going, Mr. Kloss?"

"Papa. It's Papa. Why don't you ever call me that? Everyone else does." Mr. Kloss continued to walk away, but didn't send her back to the house as he had done the other two times she had tried to follow him.

"I don't know why. Mr. Kloss just seems better," replied Ruby.

"You call Mama, Mama," Papa noted.

"I know," was all Ruby replied. She started to say more, but decided instead to quietly follow Mr. Kloss into the woods.

Finally, Papa stopped and said, "Normally, I keep this private, between God and myself, but it looks like you've managed to get out here with me, so here we are."

"And where is here?" asked Ruby.

"I feed the reindeer here. I place this salt lick for them. They watch for me to come. After all these years, they're somewhat tame, but they still rarely eat from my hand. Not like that one time..." Papa looked wistful. He absent-mindedly handed Ruby some grain for her to use.

Papa whistled for the reindeer. He stomped around, replacing the salt lick and throwing some grain upon the snow.

"No wonder they don't get close," said Ruby. "You're noisy!"

"You can do better?" asked Mr. Kloss. "These reindeer know me. I've been doing this for years!"

Ruby walked away from the noise that Mr. Kloss was making. She knelt onto the snow and quietly spread some grain around her.

Two reindeer approached Ruby. They hesitated, but they indeed had become less fearful over the years. They sniffed the air and began eating the grain around her. Ruby sat still and quiet on her knees and watched. After they had eaten the grain, the reindeer eyed both Ruby and Papa as they slowly backed away.

Ruby carefully rose and quietly walked back to Mr. Kloss. "I'll bet next time we can get them to eat out of our hands."

She put her finger to her lips. "As long as we both are quiet."

"As long as we both are quiet." Papa smiled. "Oh ho ho! Yes. I guess even an old man like me can try to learn a new trick or two. Thank you, Ruby."

As they walked on, Papa reminisced, "They came very close once, a long time ago. It was almost ten years ago. Probably a little after you were born. Yes, they came close then. Would you believe I was able to use reindeer as horses on the sleigh?"

Ruby just listened, hoping he would continue.

Changing the subject, Papa said, "Well, are you going to pick out a tree?"

Ruby thought, "So that's why he brought the axe! And that's why he let me follow him!" Ruby happily started darting around to find a suitable tree for their Christ's day celebration.

It didn't take long for Ruby to find a wonderful tree. Not too big, not too small, it was just right.

"This tree is perfect, Ruby!" Papa said, as he started chopping at it. "In fact, are you sure you're really a little girl from an orphanage? Given your ways with the reindeer and the way you picked the perfect tree, I'd say you're more likely one of the beautiful forest elves! You know, one of the beautiful Älvor that live and dance in this forest!" He laughed loudly just as the tree fell to the ground.

The two of them dragged the tree back to the house. They joyfully told Mama the story of Ruby feeding the reindeer.

Mama led them into the front room which the boys, now returned from the park, had cleared to prepare for the tree.

As the boys and Papa set up the tree, Ruby danced around it, singing "I'm an Älvor! I'm an Älvor!"

Mama looked at Ruby with a mirth-filled glance. "So, you're one of the forest elves, you say?"

"I'm a beautiful Älvor!" replied Ruby. "Mr. Kloss said so!"

"A forest elf?" Viktor scoffed. "So, if you're one of the Älvor, then what are we?"

Ruby stopped dancing. She wanted to be an Älvor, but those were girl elves that lived in the forest. What could the boys be?

Ruby exclaimed, "You live in the barn! So you're the Nissen and you've come to get your pudding!"

Vic started to reply, but Mama interrupted, looking at all the boys as well as Ruby. "Ah! We've been blessed with so many elves! And Ruby, you're learning carpentry, so you must be an apprentice Nissen. Where is your beard, Ruby?"

Mama continued, "And pudding? Ah, yes, we must have pudding. Let me go get it. And I'll bet there is a surprise almond in the pudding somewhere!"

Everyone headed for the dining room and the joyful afternoon continued. After a wonderful meal, Mama, the boys, and Ruby all re-entered the front living area of the house. Papa disappeared, certainly to prepare the presents for the evening.

They decorated the tree with candles and beautifully crafted, brightly painted, wooden chains. The boys had proudly made the chains from fine woods rather than traditional paper.

Mama and the children began to dance around the tree, merrily singing and playing instruments to the tune of the traditional Norwegian song that signaled Papa's entry. As they sang, Papa came in with a bag of presents, set it down, and took turns dancing around the tree as well.

'På låven sitter nissen'
(In a barn sits the Nissen)

In a barn sits the Nissen with his Christ's day treat.
It's good and sweet; it's good and sweet.
He nods his head and then he smiles, for he is glad,
'cause Christ's day pudding is for him to eat!

Around him are the little mice, who want some,
so they all come, so they all come.
And a bit of that sweet pudding would be so nice,
so they dance 'round Nissen in a ring.

But Nissen sees the mice and holds his big spoon high,
He grips his bowl, and says "Good-bye!"
"For on this day this treat is mine, it's not for you.
I won't share pudding with you now at all!"

But happy are the hopping mice, who dance more,
and they glance more, and they prance more.
And they're skipping and they're twirling
while their tails swing,
as they dance 'round Nissen in a ring.

But Nissen, now unhappy, bounces up to say,
"I'll get the cat, to chase you 'way!"
The cat arrives, the mice realize, it's time to leave,
the cat is getting much too near their ring!

Still playing they keep dancing and
they squeak some,
then they peek some, then they 'eek' some.
Then they get their feet a-running
'cause the cat's come,
so it's one, two, three and they are gone!

Laughing, everyone tightly grasped and then released each others hands as they stopped dancing around the tree. Papa began merrily giving out gifts to each boy. There were fruit and nut baskets, brightly colored candy brittle, pencil boxes, some new clothing, and special tools so they could make better toys.

After he gave each boy a present, Papa warmly embraced them with a hug.

Then it was Ruby's turn. Papa turned toward where she had been sitting and said, "I have something special tonight..."

Ruby's seat was empty.

Papa looked concerned, but a couple of the boys snickered. Papa and Mama walked into the dining room, where they saw Ruby returning from the barn.

Ruby looked embarrassed, but said, "We forgot to put a bowl of pudding in the barn for the Nissen. I was carrying it out to him."

"I see," said Mama. "Papa, give me the special present."

"But I wanted to give it to her," protested Papa.

Mama whispered, "Papa, she's like a little reindeer. And you're still too noisy."

Papa handed Mama a small object and returned to the main room. Mama approached Ruby quietly.

Mama held out a small, beautifully decorated and painted glass ball, with a hook on its top. "Here, this is for you."

"Why are you giving me this? What is it?" asked Ruby.

Mama replied, "Papa calls it a 'Christ's day Promise'. He gives one to me every year. He sometimes gives Promises to the boys as well, but this one he made especially for you. Shake the glass ball and listen."

Ruby admired the beautifully decorated glass ball and shook it next to her ear. She heard the slight rustle of something within. "But what's the promise? I don't understand."

Mama explained, "Papa writes a promise on paper and puts it in the glass ball. We agreed that your Promise says 'You will never be alone.' You will always have a place here with us, if you want it, Ruby."

Ruby looked back toward the main room and saw Mr. Kloss peeking in. He quickly turned away.

"Ok," said Ruby.

Slowly, Mama led Ruby back into the large front room. Papa and the boys watched quietly as Ruby retook her seat.

Papa jumped up and held out Ruby's coat. "Look, Ruby! Mama put in a new lining! You'll stay much warmer, now…"

Mama interrupted. "Papa. I think it's time for prayers and praises now."

Everyone gathered close to the tree and began to share their stories of the past year and their prayers for the next one.

Ruby held her Promise tightly and sat silently, listening to the boys as they described their hopes and dreams. Here there was no teasing. Here, she could see the true thoughts within their hearts.

Daniel said, "It's going to be hard leaving in the spring, Papa. I know you say 'I already know all you can teach'. And I'm almost seventeen. It's time I went out on my own to find work. But you've been so good to me – to take me in, what, almost six years ago now? I pray that I'll be as good a carpenter as you think I can be."

It was quiet for a while after that, but finally Christopher proudly listed what he had learned during the year, and Peter described a beautiful day he had hiked in the forest. After most of the boys had chimed in, Mama quietly said, "You boys have been wonderful for us, and you all know that. It was so lonely here before you came. And now Papa has boys to teach. And we can give toys to children in need every year. What can be better than that?"

Papa finally spoke again. "Ruby, normally Rolf would go with me for the gift giving on Christ's day because he's the newest boy. But since I've decided to go to your orphanage, he graciously agreed that you should be the one to go."

The other boys expressed their surprise with silence. As one, they thought, "The newest boy always goes with Papa!"

Rolf broke the silence by saying, simply, "I can go next year."

Ruby was shocked, never expecting that Mr. Kloss would take her. All she could think of to say to Rolf was "Thank you, fellow elf!"

Ruby noticed the boys had started smiling and elbowing each other. "He's not my boyfriend!" she blurted out, causing Rolf to blush.

Viktor started a rhyme about Ruby and Rolf sharing pudding in the barn. Christopher and Leif tried to figure out lines so they could join in.

Mama spoke up to calm down the ruckus. "Let's get back to prayers and praises. The evening should be for the Christ child, not for teasing."

Her quiet but firm words worked. The rest of the evening was spent in quiet contemplation of the tree, the candles, the chains of their lives together, and the promises between them.

The evening finally ended as everyone went to find their bed. As Ruby contentedly pulled the covers up to her neck, she realized that this night had been one of the happiest of her life.

JOURNEY

With Christ's day only four days away, Ruby prepared for the trip back to her orphanage. The boys had loaded the sleigh with so many toys that it was close to overflowing. They stood in a close ring talking to Papa, who was already sitting in the sleigh. Ruby watched the boys, noting that they were quietly blocking her entry. She sighed, seeing the teasing wasn't over even though it was almost Christ's day.

Still, she looked forward to giving toys at her orphanage, so she quickly pushed through the boys and stood next to the sleigh.

The boys had borrowed the blacksmith's horses and had hitched them up. Ruby wondered once again why Mr. Kloss didn't own any horses of his own, but always borrowed them from the blacksmith down the way.

Mr. Kloss helped her aboard, and they were off.

It was a sunny, warm day, slightly above freezing. Papa and Ruby stopped for lunch while the horses drank from a stream nearby.

As they prepared to continue on their journey, Papa removed a toy from a small bag that he had packed himself. He handed it to Ruby as he started the sleigh down the path.

"Who is this toy for, Mr. Kloss?" asked Ruby.

"Papa, call me Papa," he replied, as he always did to Ruby's questions. "There's a sick boy in a village on the way to your orphanage. His parents sent me a letter asking if I could spare a toy for him. I thought we should visit him given we are down this way."

Ruby marveled at the toy Mr. Kloss had removed from the bag. It was like one of those new machines that could fly in the air. "An aeroplane," she thought. Surely this would delight the sick boy!

Mr. Kloss watched her admire the toy, and applauded her approval with one of his large laughs. Ruby enjoyed hearing Mr. Kloss laugh. She settled in contentedly for the ride to the boy's house.

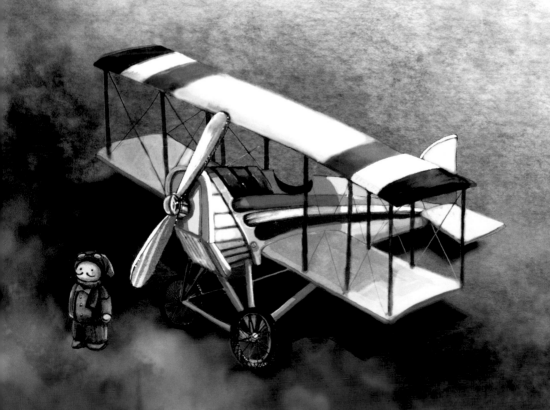

When they arrived, the house seemed small and silent. Papa went to knock at the door and was quietly greeted. After a few moments, Papa walked back to the sleigh, still carrying the toy. "What's wrong?" asked Ruby.

"They wrote me because they believed the little boy might not see another Christ's day." Papa replied. "They thought a toy might make him happy. But I was too late." His heart broken, Papa's eyes filled with tears.

Ruby touched him on the shoulder. "It's all right, Mr. Kloss. It's alright."

Papa said, "No, Ruby, it isn't all right. Some children need so much more than toys. They need love every day, they need tender care, like that poor boy's parents provided. Presents only make children happy for a while."

Ruby responded, "But making people happy is important. Everyone likes us giving the toys to them!"

Papa smiled sadly. "Yes, Ruby, what we do is important. We give children love at least one day a year. We give gifts on Christ's day, because I believe that is what God wants me to do. I just wish I could help some child every day, to make sure they receive all the love and care they need."

"You help the boys every day!" exclaimed Ruby. "Everyone likes you, Mr. Kloss!"

Mr. Kloss didn't reply, but simply urged the horses down the road. After a while, he quietly said, "Mr. Kloss."

Without looking at Ruby, he again asked, "Why don't you call me Papa like everyone else does?"

Ruby watched Mr. Kloss as he continued to guide the sleigh. She did not reply at first. After a while, she tugged at his sleeve. He turned to her and saw that her eyes were as large as saucers. Ruby almost whispered her response. "Do you really want to know? It's scary."

Mr. Kloss simply nodded and stopped the sleigh. He wrapped his coat tighter around himself, and adjusted Ruby's around her neck. Even with the nice weather, it now seemed colder. Ruby turned away from him and stared into the snow covered landscape.

Ruby began, "I never knew my Mama. But Papa was always there, until... well, it was when I was five, I think; I'm not sure. Papa was by the river, doing something... I don't quite know what he was doing. What I do remember is that Papa got hurt, really, really bad, on his head I think."

"Papa came to where I was playing. I asked him if he was hurt bad, and Papa said, 'Yes, Ruby, I'm hurt pretty bad.'"

"He said we needed to get a doctor, so we started walking toward the village. Papa tried to take my hand as we walked, but I was still playing and skipping next to him. I saw him smile and say softly to me, 'sing me a song, Ruby, sing me a song.'"

"I didn't know what to sing, so I sang one of those little children songs, one of the few I knew."

"Papa got real tired and sat down on the ground. I heard him say to himself, 'I can't quit now. I must keep going, for Ruby.'"

"I didn't know what was about to happen, but he seemed upset, so I got upset too, and I said 'Papa, keep going' just like he had been saying."

"Papa looked at me and knew I was about to cry. He closed his eyes for a minute, then he opened them and he looked up into the sky. Then, he stared me straight in the eye and said, 'Ruby, lead the way, and I promise I'll follow you as soon as I can.'"

"He took me in his arms and hugged me, really, really hard. I ran on ahead toward the village, trying to do what he said. I waited for him at the main road, so he could follow, and hoping someone would see me. I kept looking for him to follow, like he said he would. He never followed me."

"More things happened after that, but everything gets really fuzzy in my head. Anyway, I do know that people grabbed me and that's how I ended up by myself in the orphanage."

Ruby was very quiet for a while. "I try not to think about it too much. I've never told this to anyone, Mr. Kloss."

"If I ever called anyone else Papa, it would remind me that my Papa didn't keep his promise to me. It would remind me how he left me all alone."

Mr. Kloss started to put his arm around Ruby, but she shrugged it away. As the years of keeping the story to herself rose up within her, she suddenly started sobbing in the sleigh.

Mr. Kloss also had tears in his eyes, and again tried to give Ruby a hug so she could share her pain with him. Ruby again pushed him away as she continued to cry. Mr. Kloss looked out upon the snowy landscape and spied two reindeer in the distance. They looked at him, almost as if to say, "So, what do you do now?"

The next few days brought back Ruby's happiness. They cheerfully gave out toys as they traveled through each village. The children they met had heard of Santa Kloss; his arrival was greeted joyfully with awe and cheers. Papa and Ruby basked in the joy of giving as they traveled to Ruby's orphanage.

When they arrived at her orphanage, Ruby was greeted as a heroine. It was a big change from how alone she had felt when she lived there, and also different from the teasing at Mr. Kloss's house.

When she helped give the toys, she felt important and liked by those she had left behind at the orphanage.

As they traveled back to Papa's village, Ruby said to Mr. Kloss, "Now maybe the other children will like me."

Mr. Kloss thought for a moment, and then said, "Is that why you give presents, Ruby? So they'll like you?"

"Well, isn't that why we give out presents?" asked Ruby.

"Hmm," said Mr. Kloss. "Well, I give out presents because I like the children, not so they'll like me."

The long trip home was tiring. Ruby was already asleep when they finally arrived. Papa started to lift her sleeping form out of the sleigh, but when Mama came out to join them, he asked Mama to carry her inside to bed.

As Mama and Ruby disappeared into the house, Papa looked at the empty bags that had contained wondrous toys. He picked up the small bag that still held the lonely aeroplane.

"Dream about the good parts of the journey, Ruby," Papa whispered. "Keep in mind the smiling faces, the toys, and how we make children's lives happier. I believe that's what God would want us to remember."

A PRESENT FOR SANTA

Spring brought a daily routine. Ruby filled her time with school lessons, working in the shop, helping Mama, and running errands. She sometimes played in the open village center, but more often she played by herself in the woods behind the house.

Ruby knew she was now more accepted as a carpenter and family helper, but she still felt left out whenever the boys got together for fun or games. They still teased her, especially when she tried to play with them.

The village was holding its spring archery contest and Ruby wanted to compete. "I was in an archery contest in the village where my orphanage is," she declared, to show that she should be allowed to join them.

"Girls don't do archery," Viktor replied. "What did you do, pretend to be a boy so they'd let you try?"

Ruby's silence told the boys that Viktor was right. Leif took off his big cap and put it on Ruby's head. Peter took off his coat and put it on Ruby's shoulders. "Ruby's a boy! Ruby's a carpenter boy!" laughed Christopher.

"Don't touch me! Don't ever touch me!" Ruby threw the coat and cap onto the ground and ran from the park.

The other boys laughed while Peter sighed. "Looks like too much pepper in our food tonight, for sure."

Ruby ran into the empty toyshop and began pounding nails into a bench she had been building.

A bit later, Cupid walked into the toyshop. "I'll shoot bows and arrows with you, Ruby. I love bows and arrows, but I'm still not very good at them. You were in a contest, maybe you could teach me a little. We could go practice in the forest."

"We're supposed to do archery in the park so the grown-ups can see how we are doing. Why didn't you say something when I was in the park? All you boys ever do is tease me and leave me out!"

"You're not the only one who's teased. I mean, look at me. I'm the shortest boy, and they call me Cupid. That's about being a baby with wings." Cupid and Ruby both looked at the bow and arrows Cupid had placed on Ruby's work area.

"Maybe Mama will watch us," smiled Ruby.

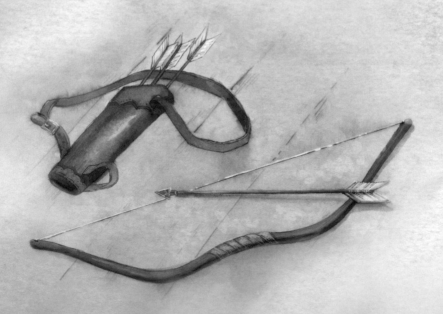

It was late spring when Daniel called out to the forest, "Ruby! Little elf! Come out front and say good-bye. My carriage is here."

"We'll miss you so much, Daniel," said Mama. "But there comes a time when you have to do what comes next in life. Be well."

"I'll miss you and Papa," said Daniel. "I think I've hugged everyone, except our little elf. I need to say good-bye to her."

Ruby came around the corner of the barn. "Good-bye, Daniel, I'll miss you." Before Ruby could react, Daniel quickly embraced Ruby and gave her a long, strong hug. Ruby pulled away from Daniel and ran back around the corner, but still peeked around it at them.

"She'll be ok," said Mama. "You need to go."

"Good-bye, Ruby," Daniel called out. "You're in good hands here. I made Dag promise to keep the toyshop in order. And, of course, Mama and Papa take care of us all."

"She'll take care of us, you mean," Mama said loudly.

Ruby waved at the carriage as it slowly disappeared down the road. "I hate hugs," Ruby thought. "Hugs always mean good-bye."

One warm night, Ruby awoke from sleep and heard Mama and Mr. Kloss talking quietly upstairs. Knowing that they both usually slept soundly, she couldn't resist getting out of bed and crawling partway up the stairs to hear what they were saying.

"Papa, you've said countless times that giving gifts to children on Christ's day is your calling. After over ten years, why have you begun questioning your purpose?"

"I don't know, Mama. I don't know. It's been months, but I keep looking at this aeroplane that I couldn't give to that poor child. I want to be more to a child than just the jolly fellow who gives out toys once a year."

"We've discussed that, Papa. Don't you realize how much those boys in the barn need you? Where would they be if they weren't learning a trade? You give them your love every day."

"Ah, yes, Mama. But sometimes I feel I'm more of an employer than a Papa. And of course, there's the one that won't let me get close at all."

Suddenly it was quiet, and then Mama or Mr. Kloss blew out the single candle that had provided some light from upstairs and into the stairwell. Ruby carefully crept back down the steps to her bed.

"Which boy did Mr. Kloss mean?" thought Ruby. "Cupid? Rolf? Daniel, because he left? Well, whoever it is, if they're making him unhappy, I'm going to fix it!"

The next day, as Ruby worked in the kitchen with Mama, Ruby asked, "How do I make Mr. Kloss happy again? He doesn't laugh much anymore."

Mama was brushing Ruby's hair while the soup for dinner was simmering. Mama hesitated, but then said, "I think if you just gave him a big hug and said, 'Papa, be happy.', that might do it."

"No," replied Ruby. "I need to give him something. Giving a present always makes people happy for a while."

"Hmmm," said Mama. "Ok, then. You've heard the story about how Papa started giving presents, right?"

"Oh, you mean how Mr. Kloss was making a dollhouse for the blacksmith's daughter, and there were two orphans at the blacksmith's house, so Mr. Kloss came home to get more toys, but then reindeer showed up and he rode with a sleigh and reindeer all the way to the orphanage and gave away all the toys he'd made?"

"Yes," Mama laughed. "I guess that's the story. The reindeer were indeed a miracle. I think Papa borrows horses from the blacksmith every year because he still hopes the reindeer will come back."

"That's it!" Ruby exclaimed. "I'll make him a sleigh with reindeer! Don't tell him, Mama. This will be the best present ever." Ruby jumped up to check on the soup, already thinking how she'd make this wonderful present.

"Isn't fall beautiful, Ruby? The leaves have fallen everywhere! We're all going to play in the forest! Come on, you can be an Älvor, and each of us can be a Nissen! It'll be fun!" Christopher stood impatiently at Ruby's worktable, shifting back and forth ready to run back outside.

"No, you'll just chase me again," Ruby answered.

"Come on, only Leif and Viktor still tease you like that and they're with Papa in the city getting toy supplies."

"That's why I can't play right now. I'm working on the sleigh and reindeer while Mr. Kloss is away. I have to keep it hidden whenever he's around."

"The reindeer again? Come on, Ruby, you still think that's going to make Papa happy? Grown-ups aren't kids. They get sad for all sorts of odd reasons. A toy won't make Papa happy."

"Yes, it will," Ruby insisted. "It will remind him of when the reindeer came – and he'll know that he has to give presents on Christ's day. He says that's what God wants him to do."

"Ok, but you're no fun. Maybe if you weren't always busy, people would like you better." Christopher heard the laughter of the boys beginning to fade into the forest, so he started to run from the toyshop.

Suddenly, he turned and said, "Hey, what if we all helped with the reindeer and helped you keep it hidden? Would you be an Älvor then?"

Ruby looked over the partially finished sleigh and the single reindeer she had carved. She'd never get it done secretly without help. "Ok. But everyone is going to have to help me, since we can't work on it when Mr. Kloss is around."

Fall mixed with the early snows of winter. The Älvor and the Nissen turned back into carpenters, painters, and wood carvers. School lessons took some time, but once again toy making was all that the boys and Ruby thought about.

"Ruby," said Cupid. "Here's the reindeer I painted. I named him Cupid, too. I hope that's ok."

"It's really nice," said Ruby. "Now we have seven of the eight reindeer carved, and four painted. Mr. Kloss is going to love them!"

"The sleigh is nice, too," said Rolf. "I can't believe the detail you put into it and into the three reindeer you carved. You have to show me how you get the carving so perfect."

"Everyone! Papa's back!" called Peter. Everyone handed their reindeer to Dag and he rushed them upstairs into the boy's sleeping area. By the time Papa walked into the toyshop, everyone was busy working on their assigned toy.

A month before Christ's day, everyone declared the reindeer as finished. Each day, Ruby found some time to secretly inspect them. Each evening, she'd watch Mr. Kloss eat dinner while she thought about how she should give the reindeer to him.

Each night, as Ruby went to sleep, she kept hoping that Christ's day would soon arrive.

BREAKING THE ICE

The early snows of Norwegian winter turned into a heavy white carpet over the entire valley. Although toys were still foremost in everyone's mind, there were always chores that had to be done.

"Repair tools. Rope. Wire." Dag recited the checklist. "It looks like we have what we need to check and repair the traps."

"Bows and arrows," said Cupid.

"Skates!" added Ruby. Both had assembled their archery sets and carried ice skates over their shoulders. "We're ready, too!"

"I don't know why you are bothering with bows and arrows," mocked Viktor. "It's not like Papa will let us shoot a reindeer for food. Arrows would be useful, then."

"We'll protect you from lions and tigers!" laughed Cupid.

"And bears," said Ruby seriously.

"Oh, my…" frowned Viktor. "Anyway, you two only get to come because Mama said so. Stay out of our way while we do the real work."

As Viktor, Ruby, and Cupid argued, the other boys declared they were ready to go. Dag and Peter carried most of the equipment, while Rolf, Leif and Christopher searched and checked for their traps in the forest.

Once they reached the river, skates replaced heavy snow boots. Despite Dag's insistence that everyone stay near the shoreline, Leif and Viktor kept daring the other to go further onto the river, as the ice seemed fairly hard and stable.

Peter commented, "I wish Papa had come with us. He would have skated with us and kept those two in line."

Dag replied, "Yes, but Papa seems so distracted these days. He never laughs anymore. Maybe he wouldn't like skating now."

Ruby called out to Leif and Viktor, "Please come back where the ice is hard. You could get hurt really, really bad!"

Viktor started dancing on the ice. "Oh, poor little 'carpenter boy'... worried about me?" He fled from the shoreline a tiny bit more. "Afraid I'll break the ice?" He twisted on one foot; the ice suddenly gave way and he was in the freezing Norwegian water.

Dag and Peter immediately began to rush toward Viktor, then stopped, knowing they would fall in as well. Dag shouted, "We'll have to form a rescue line!"

Ruby shouted back, "There's no time! Hand me a rope!" Taking one, she tied the rope to the shaft of one of her arrows.

"You can't fire that accurately!" said Christopher.

"I don't have to be accurate, I just have to get it past Viktor," Ruby responded. With all her might, she pulled back the bow and lofted the arrow as high as she could. It arched over Viktor and landed just beyond him.

Viktor immediately grabbed the rope and the other boys quickly pulled him from the icy water.

Dag, Leif, Ruby and Cupid immediately began hurrying Viktor back to the house while Peter, Rolf, and Christopher gathered all their goods back together.

Viktor was shivering intensely, but as they neared the house, he looked at Ruby, and said quietly, "N... not bad, for a carpenter... girl."

Two days later, the blizzards arrived, and so did the influenza. Bad weather kept everyone inside either the barn or the house.

Viktor was the first to come down with the flu, but Peter and Cupid rapidly followed. All three were confined to their beds.

Ruby and Mama spent most of their time nursing them rather than putting the finishing touch on many of the toys.

"They could die from this, couldn't they, Mama?" Ruby asked.

"That's why you and I are watching over them, Ruby; to make sure they get well."

Ruby surprised the sick boys by always smiling as she brought them soup and medicine. Ruby also kept the house clean and made sure not to forget Christ's day. Ruby and Mama did their best to decorate the house.

While decorating the tree, Ruby carefully brought in each of the ornament boxes, but tripped while carrying the box of globe Promises. She caught it, but two of the Promises leaped from the box and smashed into pieces on the floor.

Ruby realized that one of them was the Promise Mr. Kloss had given her last Christ's day and that the other one belonged to Mama. Ruby jumped back and said, "Oh, Mama! I'm so sorry I broke the Promises!"

"Don't worry Ruby, it's ok! Papa will make you another one."

"But I broke one of yours – and it was the most beautiful Promise in the whole box!"

"I said, don't worry, Ruby… it was indeed beautiful, but that Promise was actually broken long ago. Papa gave that Promise to me almost eleven years ago… it was the Promise he gave to me the year the reindeer came…"

Mama sighed and continued. "The Promise was 'We will have our wee one…'. He was so sure we'd have a child… but I had to tell him I was too old. He was so disappointed. But, still, he gave me the Promise, and I hung it on the tree that year."

"I'm still sorry I broke it, Mama." said Ruby.

"Don't worry, Ruby, even broken promises can have good intent." Mama began to clean up the broken glass. She paused, and then said, "I don't think anyone ever intends to break a promise, Ruby. I'm sure your Papa didn't want to leave you alone."

Ruby didn't respond, but simply helped clean the broken glass. Then, she said, "Mama, here are the papers that Mr. Kloss says are inside the Promises!"

"Yes, he writes the promise onto paper and puts it inside. I already know what it says, though, Ruby, I never forget - it says 'We will have our wee one.'"

"No, Mama, that's not what it says." said Ruby.

"What do you mean?"

"It says — 'No matter what happens, I will always love you.'"

"That's your paper, Ruby, and it sounds like Papa wrote it as if it were from your Papa," said Mama.

"No, Mama. That's not it. Both of the papers say the same thing," said Ruby, quietly.

Mama's eyes filled with tears. "That man! Even after all these years, he still surprises me."

As the heavy blizzards continued, Papa decided they could only visit the orphanage closest to them on Christ's day. The sick boys were worried about not having enough toys. Papa kept reassuring them by saying, "We certainly have enough toys for one orphanage."

But things got worse. Six days before Christ's day, Papa became sick with the influenza as well.

Ruby doubled her efforts. She made trips to the local store through the driving snow for medicine and special foods to make sure Mr. Kloss had whatever he needed.

She wiped the foreheads of the sick boys whenever their fevers broke. She worked on a few toys with the boys who were well.

Ruby decided that it would be nice to put out pudding for the Nissen for several nights before Christ's day instead of just one, because the Nissen was supposed to grant good luck if he was happy.

As she placed the pudding onto her work area in the barn, she whispered, "I hope you will grant good luck to the boy elves and to Mr. Kloss, too."

Ruby climbed upstairs to check on the boys one last time for the evening and saw Mama tending to them. Ruby went back downstairs and found three mice already eating the pudding.

"No wonder the Nissen won't share," thought Ruby. "The mice get the pudding most of the time, so when he finds it first, he wants it for himself."

Ruby called out to the air, "I'm sorry if you are sad, Nissen, but Mr. Kloss is sad, too. I hope the reindeer make him happy again."

Ruby yawned, and braced herself for the short walk from the barn to the house so she could check on Mr. Kloss. If there were toys to be delivered, Mr. Kloss would need to get as much rest as possible.

LIGHTING THE WAY

As Christ's day eve arrived, Mr. Kloss was still in bed with the flu. Ruby worried that even visiting one orphanage might be a lot to ask of him, given how he was feeling.

Still, Ruby and Mama had made sure that the tree was up, the candles were lit, and some songs were sung. Papa was able to bring in gifts, but he asked Mama to pass them out to everyone. Ruby smiled as she looked forward to everyone settling in for prayers and praises of how the year had gone by.

With the wind howling outside, most of the comments from the boys were prayers that the weather would improve, or that all of them would get well soon.

As the boys finished, Papa hoarsely talked to them all. "You are all good carpenters. I thank God for bringing you here so we could give toys on Christ's day and make children happy. I've been able to do this for years now, ever since God made me aware that I should do this."

"But this year, I'm sick. This year the weather is very bad." Papa looked out the window at the heavy blizzard. As he turned back to the group, he saw their faces lit by the candles on the tree. "We should wait until we are over the influenza and the weather improves. We need to make sure we all get well."

Papa pulled out the final present he had brought in from his bag. It was the toy aeroplane; he sat it next to himself on the table. "I've seen too many times when people didn't get well."

Papa continued, "Maybe this spring we can all give the toys away together. You're the ones who make them, so they should come from you. I think we need to skip this Christ's day."

It was Rolf who echoed the feelings of all those in the room. "If you don't give the toys on Christ's day and let us give the toys instead, you won't do it anymore, ever again. You know that within your heart, Papa."

Papa turned to Rolf. "What if I do stop? Everyone retires someday. I'm tired. I'm ready to rest." A coughing fit interrupted his words. Finally, he continued, "I think I've given all I have to give."

Ruby was so upset she jumped up and began waving her nut basket. "You can't quit now! All those children depend on you! Toys bring joy. For the orphans, it's one of the high points of their year! For other children you've given toys to, they remember the kindness you've shown!"

Ruby rushed out of the room to where she and the boys had moved the reindeer and sleigh. They had planned to give it after prayers, but now was the time, Ruby thought.

Rushing back into the room, she saw that everyone had simply waited, knowing she would return. Only Mr. Kloss wondered what had caused her to leave so suddenly.

She walked up to Mr. Kloss and revealed the wonderful reindeer and sleigh. "See, Mr. Kloss!" she pleaded. "This is why you have to keep going!"

Mr. Kloss carefully touched the reindeer and sleigh that Ruby held upward to him. He sniffled, though Ruby didn't know if that was due to his cold or the gift.

"It's beautiful," he said. "Yes, they came once. They showed me what I needed to do."

"Did you make this, Ruby?" he asked.

"We all did. But it was special. It's to make you happy. It's because you have done so much for us and for all the children that need you."

Papa looked to Mama, who said quietly, "She's trying, Papa. And I think you're getting well enough."

"Well, maybe the reindeer have been sent again to convince me to go." Papa took the reindeer from her and set them on the table next to the aeroplane. "Maybe we could even fly," he laughed.

He extended his arms to give Ruby a hug, but Ruby had already run around to the other side of the table.

"Don't you see, Mr. Kloss? We put eight reindeer with the sleigh, and we gave each of them their own number of points on their antlers! We gave them little harnesses and reins. And even names! This one is Dasher and this one's Dancer. What do you think, Mr. Kloss?

Mr. Kloss's shoulders slumped as he put his hands into his pockets. He admired the fine detail of the reindeer and sleigh as Ruby continued rapidly talking about them. Mr. Kloss finally interrupted, "Yes, yes, Ruby, they're beautiful. But look at what you've done. This is my point. You don't need me anymore. You've learned how to take care of everything yourselves. You don't need my help."

Mr. Kloss continued, gently. "It's a wonderful present." He started coughing again. "But I do think I'll say goodnight now. I don't feel well, and I need to rest to get over the influenza."

"But you are going to go now, aren't you, Mr. Kloss? I know it is dark now, but you'll go on Christ's day?" Ruby continued, "Mr. Kloss?"

Papa turned to look at everyone. "Mr. Kloss is going to bed now. I'm still sick, and the weather is still bad." None of their protests could stop him from walking to the back of the house and up the stairs. Mama stood near the doorway and silently let him pass. She looked at Ruby and the other boys and simply shrugged her shoulders. For once, even she did not know what to do.

Ruby sadly eyed the beautiful reindeer and sleigh. It had been a wonderful gift. Why hadn't it made Mr. Kloss happy and show him he had to keep giving presents on Christ's day?

Christ's eve came and went. No miracles or wonders. No angels from heaven or reindeer appearing to guide the sleigh. Just a snowy, windy, blizzardy night, followed by a bit of warming and a thick fog that crept over the village's snowy valley as dawn finally appeared.

It was Christ's day.

Ruby awoke, tears still damp on her pillow.

Mama was already working in the kitchen, having walked past Ruby after coming down the stairs. She had managed to start a breakfast on the stove while Ruby still slept. Ruby got out of bed, quickly removed her nightclothes, and started dressing.

"He feels better this morning," said Mama. "But that's in his body, not in his mind, if you know what I mean."

"I know," said Ruby. "He's sad."

"Do you know why?" asked Mama.

"He doesn't think he's helping anyone, really," said Ruby. "But I think he's helping a lot."

"Hmm," said Mama. "No, he knows he's helping. He just doesn't feel needed."

Papa's large frame sounded above them. He was awake, and soon he came down the stairs. He reached the bottom stair, and quietly looked at Ruby, who had been getting plates to set the dining area for breakfast.

"Good morning, Ruby," he said. "A merry Christ's day to you."

"And to you, Mr. Kloss," replied Ruby.

The boys came in from the barn and everyone had a quiet Christ's day breakfast. Near the end of the meal, Papa turned to Mama and said, "It does feels odd, not being out giving presents today, but maybe that's for the best. It was nice for everyone to make me the reindeer, and I will always treasure them, but I think it's a reminder of what I've done, not what I should do. It's time I went back to being just a carpenter instead of traveling everywhere on Christ's day."

Ruby jumped up from her seat at the table. "No! Please, Mr. Kloss. You make children happy! You can't quit now! You have to keep going!"

He sighed and looked quietly at Ruby. "So what if I don't start again, Ruby? What would really be lost?"

"Why... why... everything!" said Ruby.

"No, not everything," replied Papa.

He turned from Ruby toward everyone at the table. "I've told all of you to remember that what we give are just things. They're toys. They make children happy, but that's not why I give the toys on Christ's day. I've done it because I believe God wanted me to show how this day is special."

"Christ's day is about love. It's about family. It's about what we give to each other, but mostly it's about our Father in heaven, who watches over us all. It's about what our Father gave to us and how he kept his promise to all of his children."

Ruby cried out, "He didn't keep his promise to me! He left me alone!" She rushed from the dining area and out of the house, headed for parts unknown.

Papa started to jump up, then sat back down and looked at Mama. The boys quietly left the dining room.

The boys found Ruby in the barn, head down on her worktable.

"We're with you, Ruby," Leif said. "What do we do now? Papa has to go today. It's just foggy, now."

Ruby looked up to see seven boys standing before her. "You're right," she said. "He has to go today. It's Christ's day."

Mama insisted that Papa put on his coat and boots before heading toward the barn. "They all need you, Papa, but you have to make sure you don't get sicker. Part of taking care of them is taking care of yourself."

Papa walked into the toyshop. Dag sat in the shop, watching over Viktor, Peter, and Cupid. They had their coats on with snow covering their boots. "Hi, Papa," said Dag. "They're waiting at the sleigh for you."

Papa walked outside. He noted the soreness of his throat and wrapped his muffler tighter around his neck.

Though it was early morning, the fog on the snow made it impossible to see much beyond the length of his outstretched hand. He walked on, and soon saw the light of a torch. A little further and he saw a sleigh, the blacksmith's horses, with Leif and Christopher holding the horses. He then saw Rolf sitting in the sleigh, toys in the back, and there, nearby, Ruby holding a torch almost as large as her, so they all could see in the fog.

Ruby saw Mr. Kloss, and said sternly, "We're ready to go to the orphanage. You can't quit now. What you do is important."

"Yes, Ruby, what we do is important." Papa nodded to Rolf in the sleigh. He took Rolf's hand and climbed aboard. The horses, sensing the tense situation, clopped their hooves in the snow, but little sound was made due to the thick snow and dense fog.

"I guess it's next year," Rolf joked. "I get to go with you, even if it is a short journey."

Papa sat by Rolf in the sleigh, but then whispered to himself, "For such a short journey, it's a long way to go."

Mr. Kloss continued, "Ok, Rolf. The snow is deep, the fog is thick, and it's almost impossible to see my hand in front of my face. We have to get to higher ground. So we head south to the high road."

Papa hesitated. "I just don't know how we'll get to the high road."

For a few moments, Mr. Kloss watched Ruby standing alone in the snow with her torch. He thought to himself, "We should wait for the fog to lift. But she is right, it's Christ's day, and I have a promise I need to keep."

Papa felt a sudden calm as he said, "Ruby, with this fog, the horses can't guide the sleigh. But you can. Will you lead the way? We'll follow as soon as we can."

Ruby stood silently with the torch. He wanted her to go as well! Her eyes suddenly became as large as saucers.

She then simply replied, "Yes, Mr. Kloss, I will."

Ruby turned, trudging through the snow and fog, beginning to slowly tramp up the road. Through the thick fog and deep snow, Ruby marched in front with the torch lighting the way.

The horses obediently trudged through the snow, doing their best to make their way with Ruby's calls and Rolf's guidance. Papa sat in the sleigh, marveling at their determination.

Eventually reaching the higher road, Ruby watched the fog slowly thin as she continued to move forward. She passed upward beyond the fog to an area where it was somewhat clear and quiet.

Ruby turned back to see the road sloping downward into the gentle lake of fog covering the entire valley – it seemed as if everything were beneath her, quietly living within the fog.

But Ruby wasn't calm. "Where is he?" she thought. The fog around her made her feel five years old again. Papa... no, it was Mr. Kloss... he had to come. She had led the way, so he had to keep his promise.

A feeling of panic enveloped her.

He was following her, wasn't he?

The panic lasted forever,

but forever was only a moment.

The sleigh appeared through the fog. Mr. Kloss called out to Ruby in a voice so hoarse that it barely sounded like his own.

"I am here, Ruby. I told you… I'd follow as soon as I could."

Ruby thrust the torch into the wet snow and ran to the sleigh. She jumped into Mr. Kloss's large arms with a cry of both distress and relief.

"I know. That's what you said! Oh, Mr. Kl — oh, Papa!"

Papa held Ruby tightly with his eyes closed and slowly repeated, "Don't cry, my wee one, it's alright."

Ruby hugged Papa while Rolf handled the reins of the horses. Now that the way was clear, it would not be hard to navigate the high road to the orphanage.

Ruby looked up and said, "These are happy tears, Papa. Now I know that none of the Promises are broken, at least not in our hearts." She placed her ear on Papa's chest and continued hugging him.

Papa looked out upon the crisp clear road above the lake of fog while he stroked Ruby's hair. "I see. Well, your friend Rolf is doing a good job," Papa said. "We'll have toys for the children soon, just as we should."

He spied the moon, low in the sky, not yet set in favor of the morning sun. A reindeer with large antlers stood calmly in front of the moon. Papa would later declare that it stared him straight in the eye and then bowed after Papa saw it.

Papa nodded to the reindeer in return, and said to Ruby, still hugging him tightly, "You're right, my wee one. None of the Promises are broken, none of them at all."

Shh! The girl sleeps peacefully.

Ah, and she dreams.
A good dream!
Her Papa is with her now.

"Lead the way, Ruby" he says.
"But where do I lead, Papa?"
"Don't I follow you?"

No, Ruby.
As parents, we teach.
We pass on the best of our past.
But we only guide for a while.

Children lead the way to the future.
They decide where the path will go.

Sleep soundly, Ruby.

Shh! The girl sleeps peacefully.

Let her sleep.
Let her remember this day.
This dream.
This life.
Forever.

'På låven sitter nissen'
(In a barn sits the Nissen)

In | a barn sits the Nis- sen with his | Christ's day treat, it's
But | Nis- sen sees the mice and holds his | big spoon high. He
The | Nis- sen, now un- hap- py, boun- ces | up to say, "I'll

good and sweet, it's | good and sweet, He
grips his bowl, and | says "Good bye! For
get the cat, to | chase you 'way!" The

nods his head and then he smiles, for | he is glad, 'cause
on this day this treat is mine, it's | not for you. I
cat ar- rives, the mice rea- lize, it's | time to leave, the

Christ's day pud- ding is for | him to eat! A-
won't share pud- ding with you | now at all!" But
cat is get- ting much too | near their ring! Still

Tune: Traditional; Margrethe Munthe; English Text: Dan T. Davis

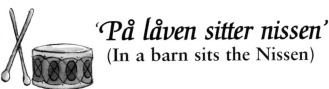

'På låven sitter nissen'
(In a barn sits the Nissen)

round him are the lit- tle mice, who
hap- py are the hop- ping mice, who
play- ing they keep danc- ing and they

want some, so they
dance more, and they
squeak some, then they

all come, so they
glance more, and they
peek some, then they

all come. And a
prance more. And they're
'eek' some. Then they

bit of that sweet pud- ding would be
skip- ping and they're twir- ling while their
start their feet a- run- ning 'cause the

so nice, so they
tails swing, as they
cat's come, so it's

dance 'round Nis- sen in a ring.
dance 'round Nis- sen in a ring.
one, two, three and they are gone!

Tune: Traditional; Margrethe Munthe; English Text: Dan T. Davis

About the Author

Do you ever wonder what you will do when you grow up? Astronaut, teacher, computer specialist, nurse, or fireman? Dan T. Davis still wonders exactly that, even though many would say he's a grown-up already. Dan hopes he never grows up – he always wants to learn, create, or seek things he's never seen before.

Dan worked with computers for many years, but decided he wanted to write stories that children would enjoy. He likes to travel and to see new things. He always wanted to go to the moon, but now thinks maybe you'll be the one to do it instead.

You are holding in your hands one of the things Dan likes most now – a book exploring new ideas and new worlds. This story is about a Santa that Dan believes in – a Santa that represents the best in all of us. This is the second of a trio of stories set in the best world one can possibly explore: the world of the imagination.

Acknowledgements

As always, I thank my wife Jan for always being there, and who is my anchor in this life. Thanks also to Akiko and Crystal, my happy doggies who constantly show me that life is something to be enjoyed.

I want to thank my Mom and Dad because they have always been there for me, and to all of my friends who have read countless versions of this story to help make it the best it could be. I appreciate your help and your love!

About the Illustrator

Christina E. Siravo makes her debut into the world of illustration with *An Orphan's Promise*! Originally from Rhode Island, she now lives in Maine where she earned her BFA in illustration at the Maine College of Art. For four years, she has sung a cappella at an Italian restaurant and loves it. She has performed in several operas and enjoys musical theatre, costume design, and set painting. In the years to come, Christina plans to keep pursuing what she loves and to continue making art.

Christina has had a passion for the arts, illustration, and children's books since she was very small, and enjoys creating whimsical worlds, characters, and sharing her gifts with children. A glimpse into Christina's inspirations and influences include: flying, nature, figure skating, funny and beautiful animations, dollhouses, cathedrals, oddly shaped trees, a balance of silence and music, and a dream to travel the world — maybe in a hot air balloon!

Acknowledgements

Thanks to all my teachers for always challenging, encouraging, and pushing me to achieve the best I possibly could. Thanks also to every one of my friends, past and present, who did the same. Reaching our destinations cannot happen alone! Thanks everyone!

Special thanks to God, for all His love, gifts, and wisdoms; Jan and Dan, for the opportunity to illustrate their story; Matthew Armstrong, for his guidance; Mom and Dad, for everything; Aunt Ann; Lucy and Jeanne; my small but supportive family; and my awesome neighbors.

"You've heard the story about how Papa started giving presents, right?"

Or maybe you haven't!

The Blacksmith's Gift is the award winning tale of how Santa decided that he should give presents to children every year.

2005 Benjamin Franklin Award
Publisher's Marketing Association
Best independently published
juvenile/young adult fiction of the year.

The Blacksmith's Gift is a real **classic of a story,** a joy from start to finish. Dan's writing **lures the reader in** and Matthew's **illustrations are truly dazzling.** For anyone who thought the art of **good old fashioned storytelling** was dead and gone, this book offers ample proof that it **is alive and well."**

— **Mark Crilley,** *creator of the comic and children book series Akiko*

The **story will clutch at your heart** and the **illustrations** are **just right**- not too much and not too little. We **rated this book a high five hearts.**

— **Bob Spear,** *www.heartlandreviews.com*

Second Star Creations

is proud to have discovered exquisite illustration talent for their children's books. Matthew S. Armstrong is the illustrator of *The Return to Narnia: The Rescue of Prince Caspian.*

The Blacksmith's Gift is his first illustrated children's book.

Enjoy this book?

Go to your local bookstore or book website and ask for these titles.
They should either be in stock or can be ordered quickly.

The Blacksmith's Gift

ISBN-13: 978-0-9725977-4-6

ISBN-10: 0-9725977-4-3

An Orphan's Promise

ISBN-13: 978-0-9725977-5-3

ISBN-10: 0-9725977-5-1

A Carpenter's Legacy

ISBN-13: 978-0-9725977-8-4

ISBN-10: 0-9725977-8-6

Second Star Creations

Inquiries
www.secondstar.us
inquiry@secondstar.us

Also, seek out:
www.blacksmithsgift.com
www.orphanspromise.com
www.carpenterslegacy.com